# THE THOUGHTS OF NANUSHKA

1/94.

# THE THOUGHTS OF NANUSHKA

Volume Twelve
*Tears and Tenderness*

Nan Witcomb

*FRIENDS
ARE NOT ONLY TOGETHER
WHEN THEY ARE SIDE-BY-SIDE;
EVEN ONE WHO IS FAR AWAY
IS STILL
IN OUR THOUGHTS*

*BEETHOVEN*

**PAN**
AUSTRALIA

First published in Australia 1985 by Nan Witcomb
This edition published 1992 by
Pan Macmillan Publishers Australia
a division of Pan Macmillan Australia Pty Limited
63-71 Balfour Street, Chippendale, Sydney
A.C.N. 001 184 014

Copyright © Nan Witcomb 1985

This book is sold subject to the condition that it shall not, by way
of trade or otherwise, be lent, re-sold, hired out or otherwise
circulated without the publisher's prior consent in any form of binding
or cover other than that in which it is published and without a similar
condition including this condition being imposed on the subsequent
purchaser.

National Library of Australia
cataloguing-in-publication data:

Witcomb, Nan.
The thoughts of Nanushka. Volume 12, Tears and tenderness.

ISBN 0 330 27329 9.
ISBN 0 330 27224 1 (set).

I. Title. II. Title: Tears and tenderness.

A 821.3

Printed in Australia by Griffin Press Limited

I can never forget,
and do not regret,
one precious moment
I have spent with you –

                    Nan Witcomb

# Tears
# and
# Tenderness

FLYING up into the clouds,
knowing I have left part of me
down there with you —
I will not be sad
because you gave me
just enough of yourself
to fill the empty space —
neither of us
have lost anything —

A telephone booth
by a raging sea
on a windswept coast
so far from me –
the dial tone purrs
'Are you there – are you there?'
a taste of tears
on the salt night air –
then through the storm,
your soul meets mine –
the words do not matter –
there's love on the line . . .

I watched the sunset
through a mist of tears
and wondered
if my thoughts
could reach across
those aching miles
of loneliness
to touch you
with my love . . . .

I stood there,
looking at the sea,
thinking how beautiful
it all would be,
if the sea stayed calm and blue
as it was that day –
I thought of you
and how your restless spirit
turns from sparkling green
to leaden grey –
and then I understood
we must endure the night,
to truly know the loveliness
of light –

Why squander
our precious now
on angry memories
of then . . . .

I felt the trust
disintegrate —
watched the loving die —
did you ever really love me —
or was your love
a lovely lie . . .

THERE you are
being you –
loving her –
here am I
being me –
loving you –

You came into my life
with your warmth
and your laughter –
no promise of staying,
no 'love ever after' –
just hope to a heart
which was lonely,
and joy to a soul
that was sad –
I ask myself
'Why am I crying?'
I have so much more now
than I had . . . .

That great black, heavy cloud
of depression —
closer and closer it descends
until the heaviness
travels down beyond my heart
to settle somewhere
deep within my being —
like a stone
weighing upon my spirit —
is it only you
who have the power
to lift it? . . .

Saying 'I love you'
does not
automatically
give the right
to invade
someone else's
emotional space –

If we build
our walls
of self protection
high enough
to be safe from hurt,
remember
that love
will not
find a way in
either —

I watch your life
falling apart
and wish
I could gather the fragments,
fit them together
like pieces of a jigsaw puzzle
to make a beautiful picture
of peace and happiness . . . . .

Forget the pride,
the pain and loneliness,
and come with me –
perhaps we'll find
the wildness
of our loving
sets us free –

If we cannot be
perfectly happy
'til we've been
a little sad,
perhaps we can't be
truly good,
'til we've been
a little bad –

Goodbye, Mrs. Plum,
we'll miss you when you go –
guess you're the only mother
most of us will ever know –
Who's going to tell young Johnny
to wash behind his ears –
who's going to find poor Billy's boots
and dry Belinda's tears –
Who's going to comfort Jenny
whenever there's a storm –
who's going to make us drink our milk
or see that Jimmy's warm –
Who's going to make us clean our teeth
and listen to our prayers –
what's the good of being good
if no-one ever cares –
Goodbye, Mrs. Plum,
they'll send somebody new
to try to take your place now –
we were kind of used to you –
the kids all wanted you to know
that you were like our 'Mum' –
I guess we'll get along alright –
but Golly!.. Mrs. Plum. . . . . . .

How sad to see
a little girl
afraid of butterflies —
I pray
she won't grow up to see
the world
through her foolish mother's eyes —

I often think
God must be appalled
at the atrocities
committed
in His name —

People
with million dollar dreams,
muddled minds
and pauper's pockets
should not meddle
in the world
of high finance –

Do we
only seek advice
to confirm
what we
have already
decided –

When dreams
become ambition
and ambition
turns to greed –
when greed
leads to vice –
perhaps
we should return
to dreaming –

I fear the law
has gone beyond
being 'a pompous ass' –
it is becoming
a vile serpent
which no longer
represents
justice –

IF we do not
fit into this world,
perhaps
we should try
to make the world
fit to live in . . . .

LET us not dwell
upon the past –
after all
it was only time
we used
to reach the present –

THERE is a time
in all our lives
when there seems
no rhyme or reason
for our living –
but if we still can dream
and hope and strive,
we may discover after all,
that life and love
are not so much for taking
as for giving –

**We** do not have to rely
upon memories
to recapture the spirit
of those we have loved and lost –
they live within our souls
in some perfect sanctuary
which even death
cannot destroy –

When winter comes,
I like to go
where yellow wild flowers
grow beside the road –
the scent of blue gum
mingles with the cold clean air
and you can see the sky
forever there –
where willy-wagtails
often catch a cheeky ride
on backs of unsuspecting sheep
and mushrooms hide
in secret places
the willows are not weeping there
but shining wet with dew,
where every creature wakes from sleep
to a world all fresh and new
and nature seems to set us free –
when winter comes
that's where I like to be –

About Nanushka —

Nan Witcomb is a fifth generation Australian.
She writes under the name of Nanushka which she believes represents the thoughts of people all over the World.

Nanushka lives within each of us, belongs to everyone and yet, to no-one — perhaps Nanushka is part of you . . . . .

My thanks to Fiona Heysen,
not only for adorning my thoughts
with her beautiful sketches
in Volumes VII – XII, but for
the music she has created
to complement Nanushka's thoughts –